EXPOSED! MORE MYTHS ABOUT AMERICAN HISTORY

AMERICANS WEREN'T THE FIRST TO LIVE ON THE FRONTIER

EXPOSING MYTHS ABOUT THE AMERICAN FRONTIER

BY JILL KEPPELER

Gareth Stevens PUBLISHING

Please visit our website, www.garethstevens.com. For a free color catalog of all our high-quality books, call toll free 1-800-542-2595 or fax 1-877-542-2596.

Cataloging-in-Publication Data

Names: Keppeler, Jill.
Title: Americans weren't the first to live on the frontier: exposing myths about the American frontier / Jill Keppeler.
Description: New York : Gareth Stevens Publishing, 2020. | Series: Exposed! more myths about American history | Includes glossary and index.
Identifiers: ISBN 9781538237380 (pbk.) | ISBN 9781538237403 (library bound) | ISBN 9781538237397 (6 pack)
Subjects: LCSH: Frontier and pioneer life–United States–Juvenile literature. | United States–Territorial expansion–Juvenile literature.
Classification: LCC E179.5 K44 2020 | DDC 970.01–dc23

First Edition

Published in 2020 by
Gareth Stevens Publishing
111 East 14th Street, Suite 349
New York, NY 10003

Designer: Sarah Liddell
Editor: Therese Shea

Photo credits: Cover, p. 1 Matanya/Wikimedia Commons; background texture used throughout IS MODE/Shutterstock.com; ripped newspaper used throughout STILLFX/Shutterstock.com; photo corners used throughout Carolyn Franks/Shutterstock.com; p. 5 Victorian Traditions/Shutterstock.com; p. 7 (top) Junkyardsparkle/Wikimedia Commons; p. 7 (bottom) Patrick Gorski/NurPhoto via Getty Images; p. 8 Everett Historical/Shutterstock.com; p. 9 SuperStock/SuperStock/Getty Images; p. 11 (top) Steve Lagreca/Shutterstock.com; p. 11 (bottom) Armita/Shutterstock.com; p. 12 Themadchopper/Wikimedia Commons; p. 13 C.C. A. Chistensen/Alonso de Mendoza/Wikimedia Commons; p. 15 File Upload Bot (Kaldari)/Wikimedia Commons; p. 17 (top) Pacific Southwest Region USFWS/OceanAtoll/Wikimedia Commons; p. 17 (bottom) Andrew J. Russell/MarmadukePercy/Wikimedia Commons; p. 18 DEA/A. DAGLI ORTI/Contributor/De Agostini/Getty Images; p. 19 MPI/Stringer/Archive Photos/Getty Images; p. 21 Bettmann/Contributor/Bettmann/Getty Images; p. 23 (Johnny Appleseed) Nesnad/Wikimedia Commons; p. 23 (apple) Iurii Kachkovskyi/Shutterstock.com; p. 25 (top) Nard the Bard/Wikimedia Commons; p. 25 (bottom) Winkelvi/Wikimedia Commons; p. 27 DEA PICTURE LIBRARY/Contributor/De Agostini/Getty Images; p. 29 Heritage Images/Contributor/Hulton Archive/Getty Images.

Printed in the United States of America

CPSIA compliance information: Batch #CS19GS: For further information contact Gareth Stevens, New York, New York at 1-800-542-2595.

CONTENTS

Words in the glossary appear in **bold** type the first time they are used in the text.

FRONTIER TALES

People have long loved the idea of the American **frontier**. They're drawn to the tales of brave settlers who traveled across North America, facing hunger, hardship, and danger to find a new home. But do we really know the truth of these frontier stories?

Many **pioneers** were brave and tough. They worked hard to survive and build successful farms and businesses. But the stories aren't as simple as they often seem. There are many **myths** about the American frontier, and it's time to learn the facts!

During the 1800s, millions of people poured into the American West, looking for land and a new life.

WIDE-OPEN SPACES

THE MYTH: THE AMERICAN FRONTIER WAS WIDE OPEN, JUST WAITING FOR SETTLERS.

THE FACTS:

Stories tell us that the American frontier was full of open spaces. And maybe it did seem that way to settlers. There were green forests, huge mountains, flat plains, and many animals.

There were people, too, but not people that settlers recognized as being like them. Thriving, or successful, societies existed in the American West long before settlers arrived. But they didn't use the land in the same way it was used in the East.

MILLIONS OF PEOPLE

There may have been more than 100 million people living in the Americas before European explorers arrived—far more people than there were in Europe!

The Navajo people were one of the many groups of Native Americans living on the American frontier when settlers began arriving. Many Navajo still live in the Southwest today.

The American frontier may have seemed unused when settlers arrived because illnesses brought by European explorers had already wiped out many native peoples. Illnesses such as smallpox may have killed up to 95 percent of Native Americans.

Others think settlers believed the land was empty because natives used it differently than they did. Native Americans tended to hold land communally, or in common. And land used for hunting could seem unoccupied.

The pioneers wanted land for individual farms on which to live and work. Many moved right onto native lands as squatters, or those who settle on land they don't own.

ON THE OREGON TRAIL

THE MYTH: MANY PIONEERS TRAVELED WEST ON A SINGLE ROUTE, OR PATH, CALLED THE OREGON TRAIL.

THE FACTS:

The Oregon Trail was a common route to the West from the 1840s to the 1860s—but it wasn't a single, clearly marked path. Travelers' wagons sometimes spread out over several miles, and people often took different trails, trying to find a quicker, safer way west.

The trail crossed bits of the current states of Missouri, Kansas, Nebraska, Wyoming, Idaho, and Oregon. It didn't go to Oregon only, but also split into routes to California and Utah.

TRAIL TRASH

Pioneers traveling on the Oregon Trail dumped a ton of trash! They left behind empty food barrels, broken wagon parts, dead animals, and many other objects.

OREGON NATIONAL HISTORIC TRAIL

More than 250,000 people traveled the Oregon Trail from the 1840s to the 1860s. A national historic trail follows the most common route today.

THE MYTH: MOST PIONEERS TRAVELED THE OREGON TRAIL IN HORSE-DRAWN CONESTOGA WAGONS.

THE FACTS:

The Conestoga wagon was a large wagon with its floor curled up at both ends. It's commonly featured in scenes of the American frontier. However, it wasn't a good way to travel far over bumpy roads.

Most travelers heading west on the Oregon Trail used smaller, lighter wagons called **prairie** schooners. A schooner is a type of ship. Prairie schooners had white cloth coverings that some people thought looked like sails.

CONESTOGA WAGON

Riding in a prairie schooner was so bumpy that many settlers chose to walk alongside the wagons!

SCHOONERS ON THE MOVE

Most prairie schooners were about 10 feet (3 m) long and 4 feet (1.2 m) wide. With the help of oxen or mules, they traveled about 15 to 20 miles (24 to 32 km) a day.

THE MYTH: NATIVE AMERICAN ATTACKS WERE A HUGE DANGER TO PIONEERS HEADING WEST ON THE OREGON TRAIL.

THE FACTS:

Many movies about the American frontier show Native American attacks on settlers. There were many dangers on the trip west, but attacks by native groups weren't even close to the worst.

Native American attacks on pioneers caused fewer than 400 of the **estimated** 20,000 deaths on the Oregon Trail between 1840 and 1860. Most deaths were due to illness. However, pioneers were responsible for killing about 400 natives along the trail.

Many of the Native Americans along the Oregon Trail traded goods and supplies with the pioneers. Some served as guides for the newcomers.

MANY PEOPLES

THE MYTH: ALL NATIVE AMERICANS ON THE AMERICAN FRONTIER SHARED A CULTURE.

THE FACTS:

There were hundreds of native groups in the United States in the mid-1800s, and many different Native American cultures were on the frontier. The pioneers met natives with different types of homes, languages, foods, clothing, and ways of life as they were passing through their lands.

Among the native peoples who lived on the land crossed by the Oregon Trail were the Cheyenne, Pawnee, Shoshone, Sioux, Kiowa, Crow, Ute, and Paiute peoples.

NATIVES NOW

Some stories and movies make it sound as if Native Americans are a people of the past. This isn't true! About 5.2 million people in the United States today are at least part Native American.

SHOSHONE PEOPLE TODAY

SHOSHONE PEOPLE, 1860s

Today, the US government recognizes more than 500 Native American tribes, and there are many other groups, too. These peoples are working hard to keep their cultures alive.

Plains Indians, such as the Sioux shown here, used tepees because they could be transported from place to place easily.

Movies about the frontier often show Native Americans living in tepees, or cone-shaped tents, and hunting with bows and arrows. The peoples of the Great Plains did often live this way, but different groups had their own ways of life.

Plains peoples usually used tepees when traveling. Some also lived in earth lodges in **permanent** villages. The Paiute people tended to make homes of brush, or small branches, called wickiups. Today, most Native Americans live in houses and apartments like Americans of other cultures.

PAIUTE WICKIUPS

THE CALL OF GOLD

THE MYTH:

THE FIRST GOLD RUSH IN THE UNITED STATES STARTED IN THE 1840S, WHEN GOLD WAS DISCOVERED IN CALIFORNIA.

THE FACTS:

The California gold rush wasn't the country's first—or even second—gold rush. In the early 1800s, a gold rush began in North Carolina after a boy found a gold nugget. In 1828, another gold rush started in Georgia.

The most famous discovery occurred at Sutter's Mill in 1848, near the Sacramento River in California. While building a sawmill for John Sutter, carpenter James Marshall found gold. The two men tried to keep it secret, but people soon found out.

A GLITTERING FIND

Conrad Reed, 12 years old, found the gold that started the North Carolina gold rush. It weighed 17 pounds (8 kg). His family used it as a doorstop before they knew what it was!

The California gold rush is the best-known US gold rush. Tens of thousands of people headed for the West Coast, hoping to strike it rich.

JOHNNY APPLESEED

THE MYTH: JOHNNY APPLESEED WANDERED THE FRONTIER, PLANTING APPLE TREES FOR PIONEERS.

THE FACTS:

John Chapman, the man we know as Johnny Appleseed, did exist. And he did travel the frontier during the 1800s, planting apple trees as he went. However, Chapman wanted to make money through his apple trees.

At that time, people could claim land by making a permanent home there. One way to prove this was by growing apple trees on the property. Chapman claimed land this way and then sold it.

John Chapman, also known as Johnny Appleseed, made money by selling trees—and land—to settlers.

SAFER CIDER

For the most part, Chapman's apples weren't meant for eating. They were for making hard apple cider, an **alcoholic** drink! This was safer to drink than water in some places. Water sometimes contained harmful bacteria.

A FAMOUS LITTLE HOUSE

THE MYTH: LAURA INGALLS WILDER'S STORIES OF HER CHILDHOOD AS A PIONEER GIRL ARE ALL TRUE.

THE FACTS:

While Wilder's Little House books are based on her childhood, they also contain fiction, or made-up stories. And Wilder left out true events, such as her baby brother's death. She also never told how her family left one town at night so they didn't have to pay rent.

Many people love Wilder's characters, but they also recognize that some of the views presented about Native Americans in the books are **racist.**

SQUATTERS

The Ingalls home in the third Little House book, *Little House on the Prairie*, was built on Native American land. The family had no right to use it. They left before the government removed them.

LAURA INGALLS WILDER

THE INGALLS FAMILY'S FIRST HOME IN SOUTH DAKOTA

In the 1970s, the Little House books were made into a TV series. The show took the stories even further from the truth.

CUSTER'S LAST STAND

THE **MYTH:** NATIVE AMERICANS AMBUSHED GEORGE ARMSTRONG CUSTER IN THE BATTLE OF THE LITTLE BIGHORN IN 1876.

THE FACTS:

In 1868, Native Americans made an agreement with the United States to stay in the Black Hills of present-day South Dakota and Wyoming. However, when gold was found there, the government decided to force the natives onto **reservations.**

In order to do that, Lieutenant Colonel Custer planned a surprise attack on a Sioux village. However, his men were no match against the Native American warriors. Custer and more than 200 soldiers were killed.

The death of Custer and his men made many white Americans angry. They didn't consider that the Native Americans, including Sioux, Cheyenne, and Arapaho, were fighting for their homes.

CUSTER IN CLASS

Custer attended the US Military Academy at West Point. He **graduated** last in his class.

FRONTIER FACT AND FICTION

There have been so many stories told about the American frontier that it can be tough to separate fact from fiction. Sometimes, people don't want to know the truth. They like the stories better.

History isn't simple. There's always more than one side to a story. There are many untrue stories about the American frontier, but there are also stories that are both interesting and based in truth. Think about what you read, **research**, and find the facts!

By the end of the 1800s, so many settlers had moved west that the American frontier could no longer be called a frontier.

GLOSSARY

alcoholic: containing alcohol, a clear liquid used in medicines and some drinks

ambush: to attack from a hiding place

culture: the beliefs and ways of life of a group of people

estimate: having to do with a careful guess about an answer based on the known facts

frontier: a part of a country that has been newly opened for settlement

graduate: to finish a certain level of schooling, such as college

myth: a story believed by many people that is not true

permanent: meant to last a long time

pioneer: one of the first American settlers to travel to and settle in the West

prairie: a large, mostly flat area of land in North America that has few trees and is covered in grasses

racist: poor treatment of or violence against people because of their race

research: studying to find something new

reservation: land set aside by the US government for Native Americans

FOR MORE INFORMATION

BOOKS

Demuth, Patricia Brennan. *Who Was Laura Ingalls Wilder?* New York, NY: Grosset & Dunlap, 2013.

Morley, Jacqueline. *You Wouldn't Want to Be an American Pioneer! A Wilderness You'd Rather Not Tame.* New York, NY: Franklin Watts, 2013.

West, David. *Lots of Things You Want to Know About Plains Indians...and Some You Don't!* Mankato, MN: Smart Apple Media, 2016.

WEBSITES

Little House on the Prairie History
littlehouseontheprairie.com/category/learning/history-learning/
Learn more about Laura Ingalls Wilder, her books, and frontier history.

Native American Facts for Kids
www.native-languages.org/kids.htm
This website, run by a group devoted to preserving Native American languages, contains valuable information.

Westward Expansion: Daily Life on the Frontier
www.ducksters.com/history/westward_expansion/daily_life_on_the_frontier.php
Learn more about the life of pioneers, and take a quiz.

INDEX